WHEN SPARKS FLY

When Sparks Fly

Iola Jôns

A translation by
Mairwen Jones

PONT READALONE

First Impression—2001

ISBN 1 84323 016 X

© original Welsh text: Iola Jôns
© translation: Mairwen Jones
© illustrations: Siôn Morris

24596604

Printed in Wales at
Gomer Press, Llandysul, Ceredigion SA44 4QL

'Fire! Fire!'

Gwenno's mother was shouting at the top of her voice.

Gwenno, Lowri and Gwenno's father came running at full speed. They gasped when they saw what was burning. The shed in their garden was on fire. Flames licked up its wooden sides and sparks were shooting out of its roof.

Dad set off at a run to fetch water from the house. He dashed back with a bucketful, then another. One little bucketful at a time, back and forth, back and forth he went.

But it was no use. His beloved workshop was on fire and, try as he might, he could not run fast enough to put out the flames.

'Be careful, Dad!' screamed Gwenno. 'Don't go so close or you'll get burned!'

She was trying to help him fill the bucket with water while her friend, Lowri, watched through the window. Lowri was scared of fire and had run inside.

'The fire brigade will be here any minute,' said Gwenno's mother. 'Let me help you with that bucket, Bob.' She seized the bucket, ran up to the shed and flung the water at the flames.

Gwenno's father was suprised to see that his wife ran much faster than he did, despite the heavy weight of the water. When the firemen arrived, they took over and did all they could to put out the flames. Gwenno and her parents watched, sadly, as the fire burnt itself out and turned their shed into a cinder. The firemen had failed to save it after all.

'It's all gone, just when I'd almost finished it,' sighed Gwenno's father.

'Finished what?"asked Gwenno, curious now.

'A fine piece of furniture – something special that I've been working on for such a long time.

I'd nearly finished it . . . it's gone now, all gone
. . .' he said sadly.

At last the flames died down and the shed stood
like a black skeleton, quietly smoking.

'Do you have any idea how the fire started?'
asked the Fire Officer.

They all looked at one another, then Gwenno
and her father began to tell the whole story.

1

Gwenno had been feeling sad and miserable for some time. The reason for that was her father's smoking. She hated it when he smoked. He never played football with Gwenno in the garden any more . . . and when had he last taken Gwenno and her friend Lowri to the woods for a long walk?

These days, her father did nothing but smoke cigarettes, watch the television or disappear into the garden shed to work on his furniture project. It was no wonder that Gwenno was fed up with everything.

Of course, he *couldn't* play football with her any more because he got so out of breath. And a walk in the woods was out of the question because it would bring on a bout of coughing.

Gwenno was really very sad every time she thought about it.

Gwenno's mother was a tidy person, neat as a pin, and she liked her home to be clean and tidy too. Day after day she had to clean up after Gwenno's dad, emptying ashtrays . . . whizzing round with the vacuum cleaner, sucking up the ash . . . dusting . . . spraying air freshener to get rid of the stale smell of smoke. Every Spring she painted the walls and the ceiling so that the yellow colour was covered with a sparkling white once again. But whatever she did, the place still smelled of smoke, and so did their clothes and their hair.

Some of the children in Gwenno's class had started to make comments.

'Gwenno pongo!

Stinks of tobacco!'

This made her *so* angry.

Finally, Gwenno decided she had suffered enough! She decided that she would persuade her father to give up smoking for good.

'But how on earth will you do that?' asked her friend, Lowri.

'I'm going to chuck *all* his cigarettes into the fire as a protest,' she declared.

'You wouldn't dare, would you?' said Lowri, half scoffing.

'Just you wait and see,' warned Gwenno, bitterly. 'I'm sick to death of all that smoke and ash!'

That evening, Gwenno climbed onto a kitchen stool and reached high up into the top kitchen cabinet where her father stored packets of cigarettes. Gwenno was so angry to see so many, she scooped them out and let them fall to the floor. Then she climbed down, picked the packets up in a pile and marched into the living room where her parents were sitting. With no warning, she threw the whole pile into the fire.

'I want you to give up smoking,' she told her shocked father. 'Starting tonight.'

For a moment her father just stared, open-mouthed. Then he exploded. 'Do you realise how much all those cigarettes cost me?' he shouted.

'Probably enough to buy me a computer and a desk to put it on,' she shouted back.

10

'You're only eight years old – you don't need a computer and a desk when you've got enough pens and pencils to open a shop!' he growled.

'I'm eight-and-three-quarters, thank you very much,' replied Gwenno. 'And you don't *need* to smoke either.'

'Now, now,' said Gwenno's mother soothingly. She always tried to make the peace when an argument flared up. 'Gwenno, I've told you often enough, you're not to play with fire. What you did there was very dangerous, and you could have burned yourself. But I do see your point. There would be more money to go round, Bob, if you gave up smoking, and keeping this house clean wouldn't be half as much work for me either.'

'But you've never said anything about that before, Ann,' said Gwenno's father. 'I didn't think for a minute that you minded my smoking.'

'Well, *I* mind,' said Gwenno, and tears came to her eyes. 'I've had enough of people in school saying that I smell – "Gwenno pongo. Stinks of tobacco"! No one in this house cares about playing football with me or coming to the woods for a walk!'

She could not hold back the tears. She turned and ran up to her bedroom, where she could sniff and blow her nose in peace.

2

Later that night, Gwenno's dad put his head round her bedroom door to say goodnight, just as he always did.

'Da-ad,' said Gwenno, her voice trembling, 'I don't want you to die young, Dad.'

'Of course I won't,' he replied comfortingly, and sat himself on the edge of Gwenno's bed.

'You will . . . if you carry on . . . smoking,' said Gwenno, and the tears began to trickle down her cheeks.

'Now, now, Gwenno fach, don't cry. I'll still be here in the morning, you'll see. What on earth has brought all this on?'

'Tomos's father died yesterday,' said Gwenno, as her voice broke into a sob. '*He* smoked!'

'Well, so did your great grandfather, and he lived until he was ninety,' said her dad, doing his best to comfort her.

'He was probably just lucky,' snapped Gwenno.

'Look, what if I promise to cut down on the smoking? Will that make you feel better?'

'A little bit better,' admitted Gwenno. 'But will you promise to give up smoking altogether, very soon?' With her big brown eyes, she looked up at her father and tried her best to melt his heart.

'All right, all right. Just go to sleep now, there's a good girl.'

'Cross your heart . . .?'

'OK, cross my heart, whatever. Now go to sleep. It's late.' He planted a kiss on her forehead and got up to go.

'Da-ad?'

'Yes?'

'Cross your heart and promise faithfully?' asked Gwenno.

'Yes, OK.'

'Say it then.'

Gwenno's father sighed. 'Promise faithfully and cross my heart,' he said.

'You've said it now, Dad, so –'

'I know, I know,' he interrupted her. 'I've promised.'

'Dad . . .'

'Blimey, what now?'

'Goodnight.'

'Goodnight, cariad.'

As Gwenno's father was leaving, her mother came in.

'Are you two friends now?' she asked, smiling.

'Yes,' the two replied in chorus, and laughed at their own timing. Then off her father went, his goodnight visit over at last.

Her mother took his place on Gwenno's rumpled bed. 'Now then, Gwenno, you musn't fall out with your father over his smoking, you know. He could do far worse than that. He doesn't go out and get drunk, and he's never nasty to you, is he? He plays with you and takes you for a walk and all sorts. The only pleasure he has is to have a little smoke!'

'But he hasn't taken me for a walk for ages, Mam,' protested Gwenno.

'Well, maybe not recently, no,' admitted her mother. 'He's been very busy at work lately, and then when he's at home he's working hard on his furniture project in the workshop.'

'That's another thing: if he's not at work or smoking in front of the television, he's messing about in that smelly old shed . . .' Gwenno was getting worked up all over again.

'Now that's enough, Gwenno,' said her mother sternly. 'It's time you went to sleep, or you'll

never get up for school in the morning. Settle down, now, and forget about the smoking.'

Mam tucked her in and kissed her gently on the cheek. 'Goodnight, lovely.'

'Goodnight,' said Gwenno, but still in her sulky voice.

Even if she and her father were friends once again, she was definitely not going to forget about the smoking. She had a job to do: persuade her dad to give up the cigarettes. And tonight was just the start.

3

'Well, did you throw your dad's cigarettes on the fire?' asked Lowri the next morning. It was the first thing she asked when the two girls met up at school.

'Of course I did,' said Gwenno sharply, and told her friend the whole story.

'So what will you do next time?' asked Lowri. 'You can't throw his cigarettes on the fire every night, can you?'

'What I'll do is put posters all over the house to remind him of his promise to cut down on his smoking. You can help me in the dinner hour to make them. Will you?' Gwenno was full of excitement about her plans.

'Course I will,' said Lowri. 'I love doing posters.'

So all that week, every spare minute they had, the two girls were busy making colourful anti-smoking posters.

'Gosh, I'm so glad you helped me with all these,' said Gwenno, looking at the great pile of papers they had by the end of the week.

'I loved doing them,' said Lowri. 'Anyway, what are friends for? You've got to help your best

friend.' She glowed with pride, and with the big smudge of red paint on her cheek where she'd rubbed her face. 'What will you do with them now?'

'I'm going to put them up all through the house – in every single room where he smokes,' said Gwenno.

'Are you going to do that tonight?'

'No, tomorrow. Once Dad goes out to his workshed, I'll start sticking them up. I'll plaster posters all over the place. He'll have such a shock when he comes in to have his lunch and sees them – I can't wait to see his face!' Gwenno's eyes sparkled.

Oh yes, there was certainly a shock in store.

4

That Saturday morning, Gwenno's father spent ages mooching around in the house, reading the newspaper and watching television. Gwenno couldn't wait for him to go out to his workshop so that she could start sticking up the posters.

'What are you up to in the shed these days, Dad?' asked Gwenno, hoping that by reminding him of his project she would persuade him to go back to it.

'Oh, nothing that would interest you very much, love,' he answered, smiling.

'Can I see what you're making?' said Gwenno, taking her father's arm.

'Oh, em, I haven't finished it yet, Gwenno. It doesn't look like anything at the moment, just a plain sort of cupboard. Actually, I think I should go and do a bit of work on it before lunch,' he said, hastily leaving his comfy chair and making briskly for his workshed.

Great, thought Gwenno. Her plan had worked. Her mother was out shopping and now that her father was also out of the way, it was safe for Gwenno to decorate the whole house with posters.

She went upstairs and into her parents' bedroom. On her father's pillow she left a poster saying, **A smoker's kiss – one to miss.** On her mother's side of the bed she pinned a poster saying, **Nicotine's for has-beens.** She was pleased with how they looked. So far so good. The bathroom was next.

On the wall next to the bath, her poster read, **Will a bath every day keep the smell of ash away?**

On her own bedroom door, Gwenno stuck a picture of herself surrounded by a cloud of smoke, and looking very gloomy. The words underneath were the insults she'd had at school. **Gwenno pongo. Stinks of tobacco.**

Carefully carrying the rest of the posters and the roll of sticky tape, Gwenno crept downstairs. On the door of the lounge she put a sign saying, **Smokeroom.** In the kitchen, the ceiling had just been painted white again by Gwenno's mother. The poster Gwenno put up here said, **A ceiling white as snow today –'til more cigarette smoke comes this way.**

Gwenno had quite a few posters left but there was one other place where she could place them. Just outside the back door was a toilet and washroom that her father always used when he'd been in the garden.

THE SMELL OF CIGARETTES, DEAR ME, IS EVEN WORSE THAN THE SMELL OF WEE!

Behind the door, she taped the poster saying, **Kick the dirty habit**. Then above the toilet, she put the poster that she and Lowri had enjoyed making most of all. **The smell of cigarettes, dear me, is even worse than the smell of wee!** By the sink she placed the one which said, **Yellow soap for yellow fingers**.

Right, thought Gwenno, I've made my point. The message couldn't possibly be clearer.

Gwenno was hungry now after all her hard work. She treated herself to a packet of crisps and a drink from the fridge and sat down to enjoy them. All she had to do now was wait for her father to come in for lunch. What fun that would be!

Gwenno grinned from ear to ear like a Cheshire cat.

5

'Sh . . .sh,' hissed an impatient woman, glaring at Gwenno. A pile of books had collapsed noisily as Gwenno brushed past them on her way to the counter.

'Oops, sorry,' whispered Gwenno, trying to stack them upright, but they toppled over once more.

'Silence!' said the assistant at the desk again.

'Sorry,' whispered Gwenno. She had never been to the town library on her own before, only to the school library, where you could talk as you pleased. Gosh, it was difficult to keep absolutely silent in this place, and for nearly an hour!

Gwenno was looking for books about the effects of smoking on the human body.

Yes, her father had come into the house that morning and yes, he had seen the posters. He had been extremely angry.

'It was bad enough hitting my finger with the hammer and having blood dripping all over everything in the outside washroom, without having to look at some silly posters as well.'

Gwenno glanced casually at his finger and replied, 'Red fingers make a change from yellow fingers, anyway!'

That did it! Her father went completely bananas – he was still dancing with rage when Gwenno's mother came in with the shopping.

'What on earth's the matter?' she asked anxiously.

'B . . . b . . . b . . .' began her father.

'No swearing in front of Gwenno, Bob,' warned her mother. He had no choice then but to go out to the garden to let off steam.

When he had cooled down enough to come in and explain, Gwenno's mother just laughed at him.

'Oh, Bob bach, just look at the state of you! Off you go upstairs now to have a wash, and change out of those soiled clothes.'

Gwenno smiled when she remembered what he would see in the bathroom – more posters, and then there would be more explosions. She listened to her father's footsteps going across the landing, into the bathroom, and then a moment's silence. Next came an almighty roar and her father's heavy footsteps coming down the stairs two steps at a time.

'What's the matter, Dad?' asked Gwenno mischievously. 'Do you need someone to scrub the ash from your back? Gosh, you should watch your temper, Dad. It flares up like a match – do you get it? Like a match?'

After quite a lot of shouting and arguing, with Gwenno's mother trying to keep order, her father turned to Gwenno and said, 'Right then, madam, if you want me to even consider giving up smoking, you'll have to bring me the proper facts. Plastering the house with silly posters won't achieve anything.'

'Well, sorry, Dad, but if I had a computer, I'd have been able to make you much smarter posters, wouldn't I?'

'Now that's enough backchat, Gwenno Williams,' said her mother firmly. 'You've done enough today to upset your father good and proper. Quite enough, thank you very much.'

So that was how Gwenno came to be in the library that Saturday afternoon. Her father had asked for proper facts. Well, she would give him proper facts all right. Gwenno found out a few things that afternoon that would shock not only her father but her mother as well.

6

By Sunday lunchtime, Gwenno was ready and eager to face her father with the facts that she knew would frighten him.

'Right, Dad, when do you want me to show you these facts?' she asked, full of importance. 'Before or after lunch?'

Her father looked up from the newspaper he was reading. 'Mmm? What facts are you talking about now?' he asked impatiently.

'I'm talking about the effects of smoking on the human body,' she snapped. 'The important facts.'

'Oh, and how long is the lecture going to be this time?' asked her father, lighting a cigarette as he spoke.

"Well, to get them to sink into that sawdust head of yours, I expect it will take about half an hour,' announced Gwenno.

'Lunch is on the table,' shouted Gwenno's mother from the kitchen.

'Oh, what a shame,' said her father sarcastically, 'lunch is ready. I'll just have to be patient and wait until afterwards to hear this fascinating speech.' He got up, stubbed out his cigarette and marched off to the kitchen for his meal.

'Parents – who needs them?' muttered Gwenno to the empty room.

There was not a great deal of conversation at the table that Sunday lunchtime.

Gwenno bolted her food and got back to her notes as soon as she could.

'Right, are you ready?' she asked.

'Ready for what?' asked her mother, spooning the last morsel of tart and custard from her bowl.

'Oh, nothing important,' said her father. 'Just some stupid facts that Gwenno insists on drawing to my attention.'

Gwenno flipped.

'Stupid facts? Stupid facts, my foot!' Her face was flushed with anger. 'You may not mind smoking yourself to death, but *I* actually mind that your stupid smoke could be killing Mam and me as well. Just look at these pictures.'

Gwenno put two pictures on the table before them, and started to explain.

'In this picture you see the lungs of someone who has never smoked, and in this one, you see lungs that are not so healthy.'

'The lungs of the smoker don't look so bad to me,' said Gwenno's father, with some confidence in his voice.

'Oh, I don't know, Bob,' his wife replied anxiously. 'The lungs of the smoker look pretty bad to me.'

'Who said that these are the lungs of a smoker?' asked Gwenno, sharply. 'As a matter of fact, what you're looking at is a picture of a child's lungs – a child who lives with a parent who smokes!'

Her parents were quiet and pale. They had nothing to say to this.

'When you've had a chance to get over the shock, you can just read the rest of the stuff I've prepared,' Gwenno told them. Then out she went to the garden, to take her anger out on a football.

She was still viciously kicking the ball against the side of the workshed when her father came out to find her. He was looking worried.

'Gwenno, come here,' he said firmly.

Giving the football just one last kick, Gwenno obeyed.

'Ok, Gwenno,' said her father, taking her by the shoulders and meeting her eye to eye. 'I promise I'll try to give up smoking in front of you and your mother.'

'That's not good enough, Dad, because we'll still be breathing in your smoke in the house.'

'All right, then.' Her father was giving in, she

could tell. 'I promise to give up smoking in the house, at least. And before long, I'll give up completely. Is that good enough for you?'

Gwenno smiled sweetly at her father. 'Thanks, Dad. You won't regret this.' And just to encourage him, she gave him a big, big hug.

What a great promise her father had made. All Gwenno had to do now was make sure that he kept his word. She would keep a *very* watchful eye on him, just in case.

7

Gwenno suspected that her father was still smoking in secret. She could smell smoke on his clothes and peppermint on his breath. His explanation was that he was sucking mints instead of smoking cigarettes, and that his clothes smelled of woodsmoke from the bonfires he lit to clear old wood from the workshop. He always locked the workshop these days as well. 'That's in case anyone steals the piece of furniture I'm working on,' he said. Gwenno didn't believe him. She was sure that he locked the shed because that was where he kept cigarettes and smoked on the sly.

On the following Saturday, Lowri came to play.

'Why don't we go to the woods to look for conkers?' suggested Gwenno.

'Good idea,' said Lowri. 'We'll show the boys in school that we can find better conkers than them any day. Did you hear what Owain Huws said? Only boys know how to climb trees to get the best conkers, so only the boys can play Proper Conkers.'

'He said that? What a cheek! Come on,' said Gwenno, 'we'll show them who's brilliant at climbing trees. We'll find whoppers, and serve the boys right for boasting.'

The two girls were full of it.

'Will you come with us to look for conkers, Dad?' Gwenno asked.

'Not today, love, I'm . . .' but he failed to finish his sentence.

'. . . busy in the workshop,' chanted Gwenno. 'Oh, Dad, please, please,' said Gwenno in her sweetest, cutest little-girl voice, 'my favorite daddy.'

'Sorry, Gwenno, not today,' said her father. 'I've nearly finished this piece now. All it needs is a coat of varnish and it will be done.'

'Hmmph!' said Gwenno, sulkily. 'I expect you'll be too busy to come to my birthday party next week as well. Come on, Lowri, let's go on our own to the woods.'

And off they went, carrying a basket huge enough to hold the biggest conkers in the world.

The two girls loved coming to the woods to play hide-and-seek. It was brilliant to have a place like this so close to Gwenno's house.

'Gosh, look at the size of the conkers on that tree,' said Lowri, staring at the branches above them.

'They're as big as potatoes,' said Gwenno, stretching to see if she could reach any.

'I'm too short,' said Lowri.

'Me too,' grumbled Gwenno.

'Why don't you try standing on my shoulders?'
suggested Lowri.

Poor Lowri! Gwenno's weight on her shoulders
made her legs buckle. Gwenno tugged at a cluster
of conkers and held on, just as Lowri's legs were
giving way. Suddenly, the branch came away in
Gwenno's hand and the two girls fell in a heap
onto the leafy ground.

'You okay, Gwenno?'

'Yes. I'm fine. And you?'

Both started to laugh and then they began to
throw leaves at each other. It was mad. Lowri had
leaves sticking out from her hair like a crown.

'Right, I'm going to climb up and get those massive conkers,' said Lowri bravely.

'Throw them down and I'll catch them in the basket,' offered Gwenno.

Lowri was actually a very good climber. She was up that tree in no time, just like a squirrel. She picked a big, prickly conker and threw it down.

'Catch!' she shouted.

Gwenno dashed forward and held out the basket. Perfect shot!

'Yes! That's one to me. Throw another one,' shouted Gwenno.

The next one didn't make it to the basket.

'Hurray, that's one-all,' shouted Lowri.

And so the game went on. Lowri climbed further and further up the branches of the horse chestnut until there were no more conkers on the tree.

'We've got enough conkers now to take on every boy in the school,' said Gwenno, looking proudly at the basket overflowing with prickly conker shells. 'You can come down from there now, Lowri.'

'Um, I don't think I can,' said Lowri shakily. 'I'm stuck.'

'What do you mean, "stuck"?' asked Gwenno.

'I'm stuck. I can't come down. The branch next to me is broken and I can't reach the next one down,' Lowri explained.

'Don't mess about, Lowri,' said Gwenno, who still thought it was part of their game. 'You're always teasing, you are, Lowri Roberts.'

'How many times do I have to tell you –I'M STUCK AND I CAN'T COME DOWN!' yelled

Lowri, losing patience with her friend, who clearly didn't believe her.

'Well, jump down!' suggested Gwenno.

'You must be joking. I'm much too high up,' shouted Lowri. 'I'd break my leg, you daft bat!'

'I could catch you in the basket, Low,' teased Gwenno.

'Look, Gwenno Williams, this is not funny . . . **I'm stuck** . . . Aaaagh!'

The branch Lowri was holding began to shake dangerously as Lowri leaned down to argue with her friend.

'You really are stuck, aren't you?' said Gwenno at last, realising that her friend was in danger.

'Yes, I am,' said Lowri crossly, 'and now I've hurt my arm as well.' Her voice trembled and tears came to her eyes. 'Why don't you go and get your father to help me get down from here? Go on, get him. Shift yourself!'

'Right, I'll get Dad – and a ladder. Don't move, don't go anywhere – I'll be back in in a minute,' said Gwenno.

'I can't go anywhere, can I, not if I'm stuck? Oh, go on, Gwenno,' pleaded Lowri, 'hurry up!'

'OK, I'm going. You look after the basket.' Then she realised what she had said. 'Oh, I don't suppose you can, with you up there and the basket down here . . .'

'Just go!' shouted Lowri. 'And don't be long, because I'm starting to lose my grip up here. If I fall . .'

Gwenno took to her heels and sprinted like a hare to fetch her father to the rescue.

8

'Dad, Dad, come quickly!' Gwenno started shouting long before she reached her garden gate.

'Drat,' said her father as he heard her coming, 'I'd better get rid of this pretty sharpish,' he muttered, throwing his cigarette under the workbench, 'and I'd better hide this as well.' He threw an old blanket over the piece of furniture, just as Gwenno burst in through the door, breathless.

'Lowri's stuck in a tree and she's hurt her arm. You've got to help her – and bring the ladder. Quick, Dad, we've got to be really quick!'

'Is she badly hurt?' asked Gwenno's father, reaching for the ladder.

'Not yet she isn't, but she will be if we don't hurry,' said Gwenno. She had a horrible vision of Lowri hanging from a spindly branch of the horse chestnut, just waiting, waiting.

Gwenno and her father ran through the wood, carrying the ladder between them.

'Oh, come on, Dad,' urged Gwenno, trying to pull him forward. He was struggling and out of breath what with the running and the weight of the ladder.

At last, they came to the tree where Lowri was still clutching at a branch.

'Oh, gosh, you've no idea how glad I am to see you,' she said to Gwenno's father as he put the ladder up against the tree.

'Can you . . . come down onto this . . . yourself . . . or do you want . . . me to come and . . . fetch you?' he panted.

'No, I'll be fine on my own,' said Lowri, stepping gingerly onto a rung of the ladder, and making her way down, step by careful step.

'Are you all right, Low?' asked Gwenno kindly, putting her arm around her friend's shoulder.

'Yes, I'm OK, but my arm hurts.' She showed Gwenno the graze she'd had from the swaying branch.

'A spot of Dettol on that and you'll be fine,' said Gwenno's dad. Dettol was his answer to every medical problem, even a headache! 'Goodness me, did you two collect all these conkers yourselves?'

'Yes,' they chorused.

'We've been busy, you see,' said Gwenno, proud as a peacock.

'So I see,' said her father, looking at the state of their clothes and their grubby hands and faces. 'I think I should get you two home and cleaned up before your mothers see you!' And off they went – Gwenno struggling with the basket, her father carrying the ladder, and Lowri nursing her injured arm.

As they got closer to the house, they could smell smoke. It was coming from their garden.

'Fire! Fire!' Gwenno's mother was shouting at them. The three of them ran as fast as they could into the garden and saw the wooden workshop all ablaze.

*   *   *

43

'I see,' said the Fire Officer. 'It looks as though it was you who set the shed on fire, then, Mr Williams.'

'What? Me? I don't know what you mean,' said Gwenno's father, perplexed.

'Well, you say you threw your cigarette under the workbench. Is that right?'

'Yes,' answered her father slowly.

'And are you sure that you had put out the cigarette properly?' asked the Fire Officer.

'Oh . . . I can't be really sure, no,' said Gwenno's father, realising what he had done. 'Oh, no! That blasted cigarette was what started the fire! I can't believe that I could have set my own workshop on fire. Everything burned, ruined, just when the desk was almost finished.

'What desk was that?' asked Gwenno, who had pricked up her ears at the mention of a desk. She had been hinting for a desk as a birthday present ever since Father Christmas had 'forgotten' to bring her one.

'Oh, Gwenno,' said her mother sadly. 'It was a desk your father had been making for you. A surprise for your birthday.'

'Oh, no,' cried Gwenno. Her heart leaped with excitement at the thought of her father making a desk for her. Then it sank horribly as she thought of the lovely desk burned to a cinder.

'Don't say anything. Just don't say a word,' said her father grimly. 'I'm giving up smoking for good, Gwenno. I never want to *see* another cigarette!' With that, he took a packet of cigarettes from his pocket and threw it onto the remains of the burning shed. 'And this time, I mean it.'

'Dad, this is the best birthday present ever,' said

Gwenno. 'You giving up smoking for good! I don't mind about the desk, Dad. I'll be OK with pencils and working on the kitchen table for a while, honestly.' Gwenno was so thrilled. She had two great things to look forward to now – a birthday, and better still, a smoke-free home.

Gwenno looked again at the pile of ashes where the workshop had stood. A horrible thought came to her. 'Da-ad? You know the shed, you didn't have my new computer in there as well, did you?'

Bump in the Night

Ruth Morgan

A bumper car can have a life and a mind
of its own – did you know that?
This funfair fantasy is full of comic
moments and has a brilliant chase.
1 85902 944 2   £3.50

Crab-boy Cranc

Julie Rainsbury

Cai has never been good at sport and is
shy when it comes to joining in. But his
life changes dramatically when a new
boy with bright red hair and an even
brighter personality comes to school.
1 85902 835 7   £3.50

Hero, Toffer and Wallaby

Malachy Doyle

Here's a gang of three friends who love
adventure. They are proud of their new
den, which is well hidden up on the
hillside. What a shock they get when an
unusual traveller finds it and moves in!
1 85902 845 4   £3.50

The Dragon Ring

Liz Haigh

Sara finds an ancient ring with a
message that has her puzzling. Is it a
lucky find? Will it harm her, or will it
give her a rare chance to travel to far-off
times?
1 85902 724 5   £3.50